D0564011

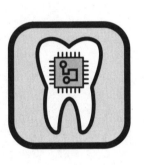

MY BEST FRIEND IS A SECRET AGENT!

Book 1: How Chip Became C.H.I.P.
and Foiled the Freaky Fuzzy Invasion

by **RICHARD CLARK**

Illustrated by **RICH MURRAY**

wattpad books **w**

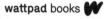

wattpad books

Published in Canada by Wattpad Books, a division of Wattpad Corp.

36 Wellington Street E., Toronto, ON M5E 1C7

www.wattpad.com

First Wattpad Books edition: September 2021

ISBN 978-1-98936-577-9 (Hardcover original)
ISBN 978-1-98936-566-3 (eBook edition)

Names, characters, places, and incidents featured in this publication are either the product of the author's imagination or are used fictitiously. Any resemblance to actual persons (living or dead), events, institutions, or locales, without satiric intent, is coincidental.

Library and Archives Canada Cataloguing in Publication information is available upon request.

Printed and bound in Canada

1 3 5 7 9 10 8 6 4 2

Cover design and illustrations by Rich Murray

For Fiona, Oliver, and Robyn

For Mary and Nicholas

CHAPTERS

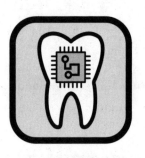

Chapter 1
A CONFESSION

Supersecret Blog #2487: My best friend, Chip, is a secret agent.

There, I've said it.

Chip wasn't always a secret agent. I MADE him one. That's right, me, Nort McKrakken.

I did it using my supersecret, supercomplicated microthingy that is so supersecret that I can't even tell you what it's called. Okay, maybe I'll tell you later. But I'm *never* going to tell Gert von Brugen from science class. (I'll tell you about her later too.)

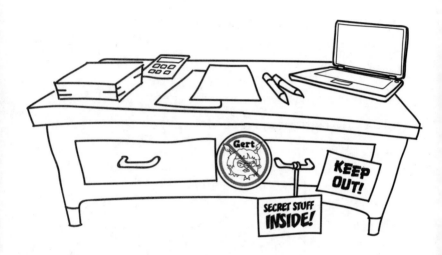

First, a little background: My dad's kind of famous. You might already know that 'cause you probably recognized my last name. He's Colonel Brock McKrakken, head of McKrakken Security Systems.

Colonel Brock McKrakken

The next step in protection.

Dad protects us from everything. That crazy oceanographer who wanted to put the whole city of Vortville underwater? Yep, Dad stopped him. That power-mad architect who wanted to turn Vortville upside down? Dad's elite team of commandos stopped him too.

Dad used to be an actual colonel in the military, so he's real gung ho about push-ups and crew cuts and getting up at 4:00 a.m. He's always wanted me to be just like him when I got older, going to boot camp and running twenty miles with a two-hundred-pound backpack on and stuff. But I can barely carry my *five*-pound backpack without breaking out in a sweat on the way to school.

I'm actually the smallest kid at Vortville Middle School. That's partly because I skipped two grades since I'm really smart. (I'm ten years old and already in sixth grade.) But I'm just small, let's face it.

But I've always wanted to make my dad proud of me, even though I knew I'd never be a soldier like him. So, I figured maybe I could use my supersmartness to help him with his security business! Maybe I could show him how to fight crazy bad guys in a supercool sciency sort of way!

That's why I invented the C.H.I.P. (That's the name of the supersecret, supercomplicated microthingy I mentioned earlier. Told you I'd tell you later.) It stands for the Computerized Heroic Incredible Person. I know, that sounds stupid—that's why I shortened it to C.H.I.P. Anyway, it's a tiny little microchip that attaches to one of your teeth, and it sends signals up to your brain to program you to be able to do anything!

The thing is, there was no way I was going to try this on myself. Do you think I'm crazy?! A chip sending signals to my brain?! What if it made me freak out or something?!

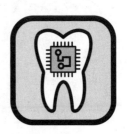

No, I needed someone else to try it on.

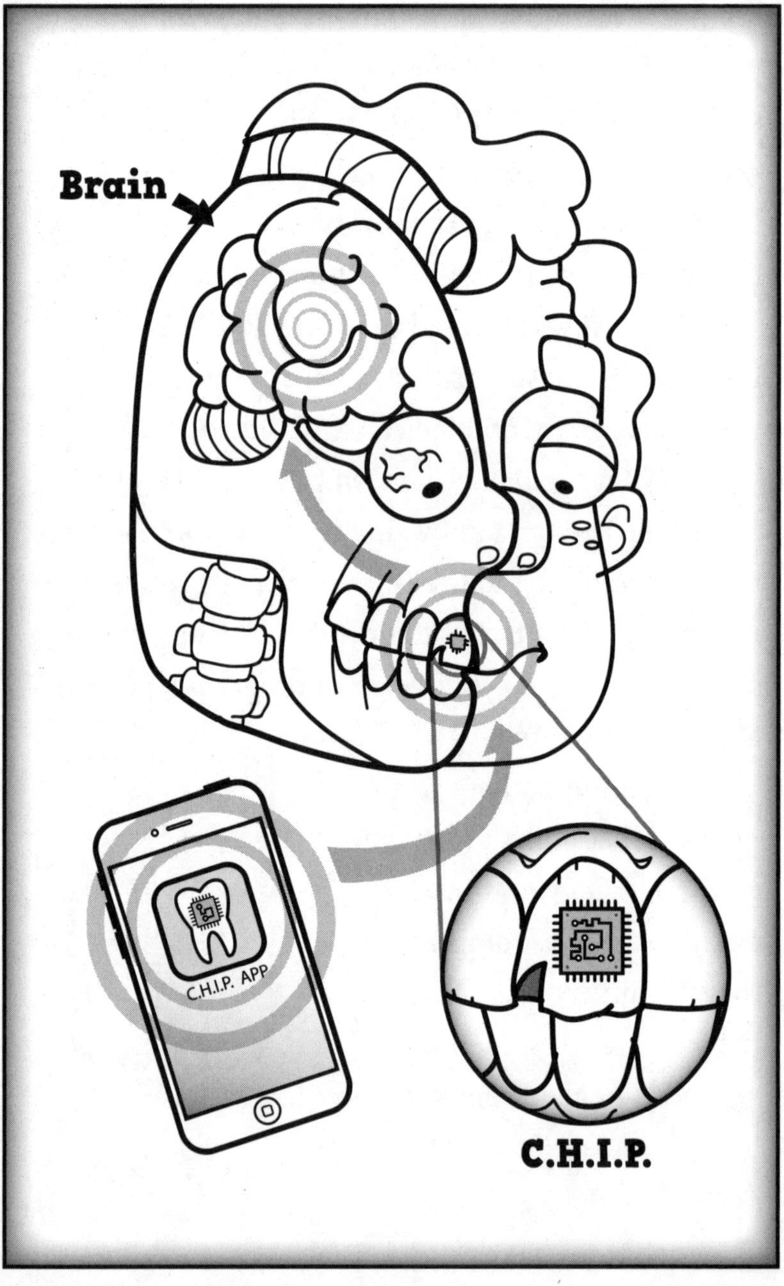
Brain
C.H.I.P. APP
C.H.I.P.

Someone like my best friend, Chip.

Lester "Chip" Munson has been my best friend since kindergarten—mainly 'cause nobody else wanted to be my friend. But Chip is the friendliest kid in the world. Everybody loves him. He's really big compared to other kids in our class, but that's probably because he got held back two grades. (He's fourteen years old and only in sixth grade.) But he was the biggest kid in our whole school even before he got held back.

But the main reason people like him is he'll do anything you ask him to.

He'll eat a worm on a dare. He'll dive into a mud puddle with all his clothes on—and with them off too. (He got his nickname, Chip, by chipping a tooth doing a crazy stunt like that.) He'll even eat a whole apple, including the core. (Yeah, a lot of the crazy things he does involve eating.)

And yes, he even tried out my supersecret, superpowerful microthingy for me.

After all, what are friends for?

Chapter 2
MY PLAN TO SAVE VORTVILLE

This is how it all started.

My dad had just stopped that power-mad architect from turning the whole city upside down, and everybody at school was talking about it. People were patting me on the back, saying they wished they had a cool dad like mine. It was a good day 'cause just the day before, those same kids were punching me in the arm.

I kind of wished my dad could beat a bad guy every day. That way I'd never get punched in the arm again.

But then Corey Smertz jumped me in the cafeteria! He wasn't as happy as everyone else about my dad saving the town because his house got

smashed in the process. In fact, my dad's commando team smashed half of Vortville while trying to stop the power-mad architect guy from smashing the other half.

"Collateral damage, son. There's no avoiding it," Dad always says. (And he says it a lot.)

Luckily, Chip was there to save me from Corey Smertz. Chip is pretty much the only kid in school bigger than Corey, so he picked Corey up and held him in the air until he calmed down. Chip never fights anybody; he just holds them in the air with their arms swinging and their feet kicking until they calm down.

I wished Dad had been able to do the same thing with that power-mad architect guy.

All this got me thinking: What if there was some way to stop bad guys without having to destroy everything all the time? What our city needed was a secret agent kind of guy, someone who could sneak into places and use his smarts to stop bad guys from doing bad things in the first place.

But that kind of secret agent guy didn't really exist. That was just in the movies.

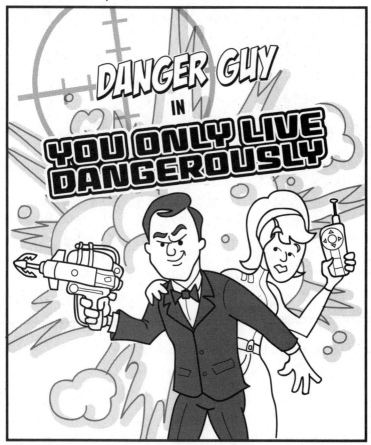

I mean, someone would have to *create* someone like that. Then I realized . . .

That someone was me!

I rushed home right after lunch, skipping social studies and phys ed. (Trust me, I didn't miss anything.)

I was pretty sure Gert von Brugen saw me go, but I didn't care. (Told you I'd get to her later too.) In science class, Gert is always trying to do better projects than me, but she never does. She even tries to sabotage *my* projects!

Gert von Brugen

So, I guess she thought I was rushing home to get a head start on my next invention for class or something, but she was only half right. I was rushing home to invent another invention all right, but it wasn't going to be for science class.

It was going to be to save Vortville!

Chapter 3
CHIP GETS A C.H.I.P.

Actually, I'd been working on my supersecret, supercomplicated microthingy for a while.

I was still perfecting it, and I was pretty sure it wasn't ready yet, but I needed it to save the city, so I figured it was time to field test it. So I called Chip.

I told you Chip was always up for anything, but there was another reason he was perfect for this job. You know that chipped tooth he has? It's actually a false tooth. He can take it out anytime! (He often does this to freak out little kids.)

So I attached the Computerized Heroic Incredible Person microthingy to the back of Chip's false tooth, and he put the tooth back in his mouth. He asked me what was going to happen when the microthingy sent signals to his brain. I told him that he'd be able to do anything I programmed him to do. He said, "Cool. And could I have a cookie?"

Now was the moment of truth. Would the C.H.I.P. work or not? If so, we could save Vortville. If not, Dad would go on saving half of Vortville while smashing the other half.

Chip and I went down to my basement where I have all my superpowerful computer stuff set up.

NORT'S BASEMENT HQ

1. Suped-Up Computer
2. Cool Buttons & Stuff
3. Secret Satellite Tracker
4. Lunch Zapinator
5. Security Camera
6. VPS—Vortville Positioning System
7. Nort-Cloud Network
8. Panic Button (don't push this!)
9. Big Jar of Jelly Beans
10. Executive Chair (set extra high)

I decided to start small. I programmed the C.H.I.P. microthingy to make Chip able to do division. He'd never really caught on with division before, even though I was always helping him, so I figured if he could do four divided by two, the C.H.I.P. must work.

When I asked Chip what was four divided by two, he looked embarrassed, just like he always does when he's asked a question in class (any question in any class). He said, "You know I can't do division—*two*."

Interesting! Then I asked him what was twelve divided by three, and he said, "Come on, Nort, stop making fun of me—*four*."

I couldn't believe it! The C.H.I.P. was working!

I decided to give him a tough one, one with a remainder. "What's ten divided by three?"

Chip got angry and said, "I don't even know what you're talking about—*3.333333 . . .*" And he was right! But then he just kept going on with the threes. He couldn't stop!

I told him it was enough, but he just kept going and going and going! I had to turn off the C.H.I.P. to get him to stop, and Chip finally took a breath. I made a mental note to reprogram the C.H.I.P.: No more remainders!

After that, I tried a bunch of other things on him—speaking French, playing the piano, bowling, and other cool stuff. He aced it all!—which was pretty incredible since we don't even have a bowling alley.

I tried to keep from hyperventilating. This was my most awesome invention ever! This was going to revolutionize my dad's security business and maybe even law enforcement all over the world!

Chip was thrilled by what was happening too.
"Wow, that was amazing!" he said. "And I still want a
cookie."

Chapter 4
THE BIG STINK

Now came the hard part: Getting my dad to put Chip on his commando team.

The first thing I had to do was give Chip a new name when the C.H.I.P. microthingy was working. Then I realized—how about *C.H.I.P.*? I mean, it was Chip's name anyway, and written in all capitals and periods, it looked kind of secret-agenty.

I was hoping Dad would think a programmable secret agent named C.H.I.P. was a cool thing for your kid to invent. But I mainly wanted to get C.H.I.P. working before the next crazy bad guy attacked.

Okay, I'm going to jump ahead a bit here and just say that it didn't exactly work. When my dad starts hearing people talk about science and computers and stuff, he kind of zones out. "Some in my line of work go for all those computing machines and fancy doodads, but in my book, nothing beats boots on the ground!" he said while doing fifty one-handed push-ups.

I tried to get him to listen: "But I invented something nobody else in the world has invented! It's the next step in national security! It's the next step in *evolution*!"

But he just told me to go do my homework. I told him I'd finished my homework for the whole school year already, and it was only October. "Then you have time to train for football tryouts. It builds discipline!"

I could see I wasn't getting anywhere with Dad.

The next day, I just hung out with Chip all day, trying out different skills with the C.H.I.P. he still had on his tooth. I got him to break down the ingredients of the sloppy joes in the cafeteria with just one taste. (Who knew they had so much sodium nitrate?)

I taught him how to dance the Watusi with just the push of a button. (Good thing most kids just thought he had ants in his pants.)

I even got him to trim the bushes by the school entrance into topiary animals. (His pygmy hippo was the best.)

But even though the C.H.I.P. inside Chip was working great, I was still feeling *blah*. After all, I didn't design it so Chip could do party tricks. I designed it to make him be the best, coolest new weapon against crazy bad guys since the Sticky Net Launcher! (Yep, I invented that too.)

Then just as Chip and I were heading home from school, we got this really stinky whiff of something. I figured it was just the school kitchen dumping leftover sloppy joe mix. But the smell got worse the farther we got from school. And it wasn't just us smelling it. Everybody on the street was starting to cough and plug their noses.

Chip and I couldn't figure out exactly what the smell was, but when Chip said, "Who cut the cheese?" I finally figured it out. It was cheese! Really stinky cheese, and now the whole city reeked of it!

I wondered what had happened. Maybe an explosion at the cheese factory?

Maybe a fourteen-truck pileup of cheese trucks on the highway?

Chip and I bolted for my dad's office, and when we got there, Dad and his commando team were suiting up for duty. It was worse than I thought—a crazed cheese maker named The Big Cheese was stinking up Vortville with cheese! But not just regular cheese, *Limburger* cheese, a cheese so stinky that its stink should be classified as a hazardous gas.

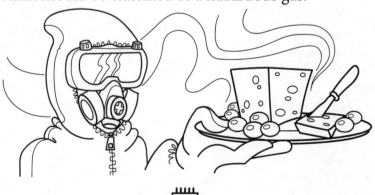

The Big Cheese wanted revenge on people everywhere who hated the smell of Limburger, which he considered the finest cheese around. He had huge gas canisters of concentrated Limburger fumes, and he was driving all over town in his Cheesemobile gassing everybody!

Who cut the cheese indeed!

My dad had to work fast to find The Big Cheese and shut him down before he gassed the whole town! But as Dad and his team headed out, I knew that if he found The Big Cheese and destroyed his Cheesemobile, it would probably blow up the gas canisters, and all the gas would be released at once!

No, this job needed somebody to handle things with some stealth, someone who could *shut down* the gas canisters, not destroy them.

This job needed C.H.I.P.!

Chapter 5
C.H.I.P.'S FIRST MISSION

Chip and I raced to HQ (headquarters—yeah, my basement), and we used my computer to tie into a military satellite. (Okay, please don't tell anybody I can do this. Especially my dad!)

Using an infrared image, I was able to pinpoint the origin of the cloud of gas that was spreading all over town.

Now it was time for C.H.I.P. to go on his first mission! But what skill would he need to take down The Big Cheese? Division? Probably not. Bowling? Don't think so. Speaking French? Hmm. Maybe The Big Cheese was French. The French are into cheese . . . but maybe not Limburger.

No, I needed to come up with a totally new skill for C.H.I.P., and I needed it fast!

Meanwhile, my dad was trying to chase down the Cheesemobile by following all the cheese fumes. He wasn't doing very well. He thought every other car was the Cheesemobile, so his team blasted them all with Slime Cannons. (I didn't invent that, but I wish I had! I mean, come on, Slime Cannons? Totally destructive, but *totally cool*!)

Chip and I were still stuck for a skill. Chip said, "How about snowboarding?!" I asked him how that could stop The Big Cheese. Chip said he didn't know, he just always wanted to learn how to snowboard.

At first, I got a little annoyed that Chip wasn't really helping, but then I realized he was onto something. But I didn't need him to be an expert snowboarder, I needed him to be an expert *skate*boarder!

Out front, I used this app I made for my smartphone to turn Chip into C.H.I.P. I typed in *skateboarding*, and BAM! Chip became C.H.I.P. the sick skater dude! But he didn't just skate cool, he *looked* cool too! He looked stronger, his hair was cool, and his kind of goofy regular expression went away. Not only that, the C.H.I.P. on his tooth had actually morphed his clothes too! He didn't even look like Chip anymore!

before | AFTER

C.H.I.P. took off down the street fast! Then I realized: I've got to follow him! So I jumped on my bike and tried to keep up. I gave C.H.I.P. directions through a two-way earpiece. "Take a left at Broadview! No, your other left!" I wished I could make C.H.I.P. an expert skateboarder *and* know his right from left at the same time.

After a few blocks, I knew we were getting close. Not only was the stink getting worse, we kept passing more and more slimed cars that my dad had blasted.

Finally, we turned a corner and there it was, the Cheesemobile itself! And there was The Big Cheese with his head sticking out like a crazy tank driver, firing blasts of concentrated Limburger stink at hordes of gagging people!

We had gotten here before my dad could, so we had a chance to prove ourselves. Through the earpiece, I told C.H.I.P. to catch up with the Cheesemobile and find a way into it. "Try getting in from underneath!"

"Yo, dude!" he said and sped up. At the last second, he flattened himself onto his back on the skateboard, then he rolled right under the moving Cheesemobile!

C.H.I.P. told me through my earpiece that he found a hatch under there. Well, what he actually said was, "Found this righteous door thingy! I'm goin' in, dude!" I was amazed at how much the C.H.I.P. had affected Chip's personality. But I also realized that his skater-dude identity wasn't what he needed to get into the Cheesemobile because skater dudes have no idea how to open hatches under tanks!

So, using my app, I made C.H.I.P. a cat burglar! Now he could pick the lock on the hatch!

But he also started to lose control of the skateboard because he wasn't a skater dude anymore! "Whoa!!!"

C.H.I.P. got the hatch open and pulled himself inside just before the skateboard flipped, getting *smashed* under the wheels of the Cheesemobile.

Okay, that was a close call. *Too* close. But at least now C.H.I.P. was in. And luckily The Big Cheese didn't notice him since his head was sticking out of the top and he was so busy blasting everybody with Limburger stink.

Now C.H.I.P. had to shut down the gas canisters, but cat burglars don't know how to do that. He needed a new skill again.

So I made him a chemist!

But once C.H.I.P. got to work on the canisters,
The Big Cheese finally spotted him and jumped him!
The guy was like, "Hands off! That's 99.6 percent pure
Limburger fumes—the gas of the gods!"

C.H.I.P. fought as best he could, but chemists
aren't really known for being able to throw a punch.
But luckily, cheese makers aren't, either, so it was kind
of a goofy fight.

Anyway, to save time, I made C.H.I.P. a wrestler next, and sure enough, he got The Big Cheese into a headlock! "I'm gonna put you through my shredder, Big Cheese!" It helped that The Big Cheese's name was kind of a wrestler-type name already.

But The Big Cheese had planned for everything. He was able to reach a switch that set off a timer for the gas canisters to explode!

"Now the whole world will reek of the beautiful, pungent scent of the king of cheeses!" he screamed with evil glee.

C.H.I.P. had ten seconds to stop the timer, but wrestlers don't know a whole lot about defusing bombs. So he bopped The Big Cheese on the head, knocking him out, and then I turned C.H.I.P. into an electronics guy to stop the timer!

And it was just in time, too, 'cause he cut the red timer wire on the gas canisters with one second to spare!

Phew!

We'd done it! C.H.I.P. and I had saved Vortville!

Just then, Dad and his commando team showed up. He pulled open the top hatch of the Cheesemobile and yanked out The Big Cheese, who was just waking back up.

The crowd cheered, and Dad smiled and waved to everybody. "All in a day's work for McKrakken Security Systems!"

But then C.H.I.P. came out holding the red wire, and people cheered even louder for *him*! "Hooray for the geeky electronics guy who can also do tons of other stuff!"

Dad wasn't very happy. He thought he'd saved the day and deserved all the credit, but the news photographers just wanted him to get out of the way so they could all shoot C.H.I.P.!

I made a mental note to avoid Dad when I got home that night.

Chapter 6
C.H.I.P. GETS FAMOUS

The next day, all everybody in town was talking about was C.H.I.P.—even though they had no idea who he was.

Who was this expert skateboarder, cat burglar, chemist, wrestler, and electronics guy who just saved the town?

Where did he live?

What was his favorite food?

Was he dating anybody famous? (Chip got a chuckle out of that last one.)

I figured all this was okay (even kind of cool!), but I told Chip not to tell anybody at school about his secret identity until I figured out the best way to break the news.

But Chip couldn't help himself. He went around school all day telling people it was really him who took down the evil cheese guy the day before! But fortunately, nobody believed him. They just thought it was goofy old Chip being goofy old Chip, and hey, how about squirting some milk out of your nose?

Which he did.

I figured this C.H.I.P. business was serious, and the only person I was going to share it with was my dad. Well, I guess I'd already done that, but I figured maybe this time he'd believe me.

But then I saw Carla Mawhinney. She was at her locker, taking out her lunch in a way that only she could do. Every movement was perfect . . . every flick of her hair a visual symphony.

Carla Mawhinney

I'd never thought myself worthy of Carla's attention . . . but then I realized that I was a changed man today (okay, a changed *boy*). Yesterday I was just plain old sixth-grade brainiac Nort McKrakken. Today I was the kid who'd saved the city!

So I went over to Carla and said hi. She was sweet, as always, but I knew she just looked at me like a little brother. Sure, I was two years younger than her and smaller than every other boy in school, but I was more of a man than any of them! While they were playing their stupid video games and kicking their stupid footballs, I was saving Vortville!

I desperately wanted to tell Carla everything, but I knew I couldn't. So instead I mustered up the courage to ask her if I could sit at her table in the cafeteria at lunch. She said,

"Nort, you're really sweet, but the kind of boy I like is big and strong and brave and amazing— like that new hero guy in the newspaper!"

Then she opened her locker all the way, and there, taped to the inside of her locker door, was every newspaper photo of Chip as C.H.I.P.! And she had drawn a big heart around each of them!

I couldn't believe it. Carla was in love with my creation but didn't even want to sit next to me at lunch!

This was too much for me to bear, so I just blurted out, "I created that guy! I invented C.H.I.P., the Computerized Heroic Incredible Person! If you're in love with him, you're really in love with me!!"

But Carla just gave me this really sad look, like I was a puppy with an injured paw or something.

Then I noticed other kids walking by, laughing and rolling their eyes at me.

I couldn't take it. I ran off and headed home early.

But there was someone I passed in the hall who wasn't laughing. Yep, Gert von Brugen. She knew I was up to something—and she was determined to find out what.

When I got home my dad was already back from work, so I decided to tell him everything about C.H.I.P. I knew he hadn't taken me seriously before, but after The Big Cheese incident, there was no way he could argue with his own eyes!

Or maybe he could. As usual, Dad wasn't in a very good mood. He had all the newspaper articles about C.H.I.P. on his desk, and before I could open my mouth, he started going on and on about this "vigilante" who was endangering the city.

"If that guy interferes with another one of my operations, I'm going to shut him down, and fast!"

Then he turned to me and said, "So, Nort, what was it you wanted to talk about? Got another crazy doodad you want to show me?"

I couldn't believe my dad still didn't take C.H.I.P. seriously. And I couldn't believe he still didn't realize his own son had created C.H.I.P. in the first place! All I knew was that if I told him, he'd shut my C.H.I.P. project down for good!

And that wouldn't just be the end of my greatest invention, it might be the end of Vortville itself!

Chapter 7
EXPLODING HEADS

Things weren't looking good.

I couldn't tell my dad about C.H.I.P. I *tried* to tell Carla, but she wouldn't believe me. And Gert von Brugen, the *last* person I wanted to know about C.H.I.P., was starting to figure things out.

I needed to take control of the situation.

Chip and I headed down to HQ. I told him we had to keep a lid on the C.H.I.P. project. That meant *both* of us not spilling the beans to anybody. We wanted to use C.H.I.P. to keep the city safe from crazy bad guys, and if those bad guys ever found out what was really going on—that C.H.I.P. was really just a kid being controlled by another kid—they'd laugh us out of the city.

Nope, as far as crazy bad guys knew, C.H.I.P. was a *real* secret agent who could take them all on at once!

This bummed Chip out because what's the point of being supercool if you have to hide it from everybody all the time?

I told him that real secret agents and even superheroes in movies never go around telling people who they really are. It would blow their cover.

Chip thought about that for a while and finally said that if real secret agents don't go around telling people they're secret agents, then he shouldn't either. He also said it would be *really* cool if he was also a superhero.

I told him superheroes weren't real. He thought about that for a while too.

It was time to get serious and perfect the C.H.I.P. It had worked amazingly well the first time out, but I needed Chip as C.H.I.P. to be able to go from one skill to another *by himself*—and superfast! So we started to get to work . . .

. . . and then Stella showed up. My sister. Eight years old and almost as smart as me. (She thinks she's *smarter*.) She had one of those stupid Freaky Fuzzy things with her—you know, that mechanical alien-pet toy that moves its eyes and actually talks to you? Yeah, creepy, but they were all over the place. Every little girl had one, and they were *really* annoying.

Stella wanted to know what we were up to. She was always sticking her nose in my business. When I was seven, I had almost figured out how to power our entire house just by supercharging the blender. Then Stella walked in, hit *Frappé*, and instead of an answer to the world's energy crisis, we ended up with banana-strawberry smoothie all over the place.

And last year, I almost solved global warming with my plan to build the world's hugest ice-cube tray. But once again, Stella messed things up by pouring fruit punch into the prototype ice-cube tray in the freezer. Who knew it would self-destruct when exposed to Red Dye 40?

I told Stella to take a hike. I was working on something *seriously* serious this time. Then her Freaky Fuzzy started scooting around the room, nosing into every nook and cranny of my HQ. And still with the questions!

This sure seemed like the perfect toy for Stella.

Finally we got rid of Stella and her Freaky Fuzzy, and I started to reprogram the C.H.I.P. to let Chip switch from one skill to another whenever he wanted.

But there was a risk. I could overload the C.H.I.P. and blow the whole thing out, which wouldn't be too cool if Chip was right in the middle of fighting some crazy bad guy. And there was also a risk of overloading Chip's *brain*, which, let's face it, probably wasn't that hard to do.

This brain will overload in 5 seconds.

Have a nice day!

I just hoped that that thing about people only using 10 percent of their brains was true. Maybe the C.H.I.P. might allow Chip to use his other 90 percent.

Or it might make his head explode.

I considered my options and decided that Chip would think his head exploding was kind of cool.

Chapter 8
MORE FEMALE TROUBLE

The next day at school, I was really distracted.

The reprogramming test on Chip had gone well, but the only *real* way to test the new C.H.I.P. programming would be during a real-life crazy bad guy attack. And who knew when that was going to happen? I mean, I didn't *want* it to happen, but until it did, I'd be waiting in suspense. And what if it happened and the new C.H.I.P. didn't work?!

This whole thing was driving me crazy. I couldn't think straight. In science class, I even forgot the molecular formula for potassium dihydrogen phosphate! Me, Nort McKrakken! There I was, standing in front of the class, presenting my latest project (a hamster-powered washing machine—I'll tell you later), and I went blank.

Nobody said anything, but I could tell they were laughing on the inside. And the main one laughing

on the inside was Gert von Brugen. Actually, she was
laughing on the outside too.

It's KH_2PO_4. **Duh!**

After class, Gert followed me to the cafeteria. I just wanted to sit with Chip and drown my sorrows in chocolate milk, but she kept pestering me.

"What're you working on, Nort? I know it's something big. You're usually only distracted like this when it's something big."

I told her I was sick of her trying to steal my science ideas and she should take a hike. (I couldn't believe both Gert *and* Stella were trying to nose in on my latest, greatest project. What is it with girls?)

That's when things got a little weird. Gert said she saw me when I was bragging to Carla before (but fortunately didn't *hear* what I was saying). "But why should you tell Carla?" she asked. "You should tell *me*! Carla wouldn't appreciate it the way I would! I mean, she probably doesn't even know the periodic table!"

Just think about the implications of this. What if Gert von Brugen knew about C.H.I.P.? She'd probably try to take control of the whole operation. And she wouldn't use him to fight crazy bad guys; she'd probably turn him into the ultimate henchman so *she* could become a crazy bad guy! The most powerful crazy bad guy in the world!

Gert von Brugen would have ultimate power, and the first thing she'd do with that power is make me her *boyfriend*!

So, I'm sure you can see that, for national security reasons, I could never breathe a word about C.H.I.P. to Gert von Brugen. And for personal reasons too. I mean—*yech*!

But then Chip did something that almost blew it for both of us. Someone at another table dared him to open a bottle with his teeth. Without thinking (when does he ever?), he started to yank off the bottle cap with his front teeth—including the chipped one! The one with the C.H.I.P. on it!

Thankfully, the tooth didn't break, but all that pressure briefly activated the C.H.I.P, and for a second it *glowed*.

Nobody said anything . . . but I think Gert noticed.

Chip and I got out of there fast. But I wondered if Gert really saw the glowing tooth and if that got her thinking.

And thinking is the one thing you never want to get Gert von Brugen to do.

Chapter 9
FREAKY FUZZIES COMING TO TOWN

"Max Schleimer busted out of prison!"

My dad announced this to me over breakfast. Max Schleimer was the power-mad architect guy who wanted to turn the whole city upside down. My dad had destroyed half the city trying to catch him, and now Schleimer had used his architect skills to sneak out of the toughest prison in the city. Apparently, he took apart the whole prison and rebuilt it upside down without anybody noticing—until he escaped and it was too late.

This guy really had *upside down* on the brain.

"We destroy half the city trying to catch him, and they just let him go!" By "they," my dad meant the guys who ran the prison. Dad didn't think "they" were tough enough. Anyway, "they" just made his job twice as hard because he'd been hired to do the security for this big Freaky Fuzzy Con on the weekend, and now the biggest threat to the whole thing would be Max Schleimer!

What I didn't tell my dad was that for me and Chip, this was perfect. Now we could try out C.H.I.P.'s new programming! Max Schleimer was toast! We were going to stop him in his tracks before he could turn the Freaky Fuzzy Con upside down—literally. This was our chance!

Not that I cared about the Freaky Fuzzy convention—I just wanted a place for C.H.I.P. to do his new stuff—but my sister was *dying* to go to the convention. Not only were there going to be Freaky Fuzzy fans from everywhere buying and selling vintage Freaky Fuzzies, but the main presentation was

Seth Mindwarp

going to be a big unveiling of the *new* Freaky Fuzzy toys. They were supposed to have tons of new features, making them almost real, and the reclusive owner of the company was going to do the big rollout.

That's right, Seth Mindwarp himself!

Stella stopped eating her Kelp Krispies in mid-chew and yelled, "It's on TV!" It was the new Freaky Fuzzy commercial. There was Seth Mindwarp demonstrating Freaky Fuzzies 2.0. Stella thought they looked incredible, but I just thought they looked even creepier than the originals.

They were almost *too* real. Not only could they understand speech commands, they could even read facial expressions. And they had 147 facial expressions of their own! They could also walk up and down stairs, sing you to sleep, and even answer your phone.

Okay, they were cool technology, but they were still just toys. Or were they? I mean, with all those new features, they had to be able to do other things. But what? I couldn't figure it out. All I knew was that if I were some kind of tech genius like Seth Mindwarp, I'd do something more than just make annoying little toys.

Anyway, the big Freaky Fuzzy 2.0 unveiling was going to go off without a hitch—not thanks to my dad but thanks to *me* . . . and C.H.I.P.!

Chapter 10
FREAKY FUZZY MANIA

Saturday morning, 10:00 a.m. The convention center was already a mob scene.

There was Freaky Fuzzy stuff everywhere. Not only were there tons of booths selling vintage Freaky Fuzzies and Freaky Fuzzy accessories, there were tons of kids walking around dressed as their favorite Freaky Fuzzy! Everybody wanted to prove that *their* favorite Freaky Fuzzy was the best.

In my opinion, it was time for these kids to get a life.

My dad and his team had been here since 6:00 a.m. scoping out the place, on the lookout for the crazy architect guy. I had wanted to do the same with Chip, but my mom made me go later with her and Stella.

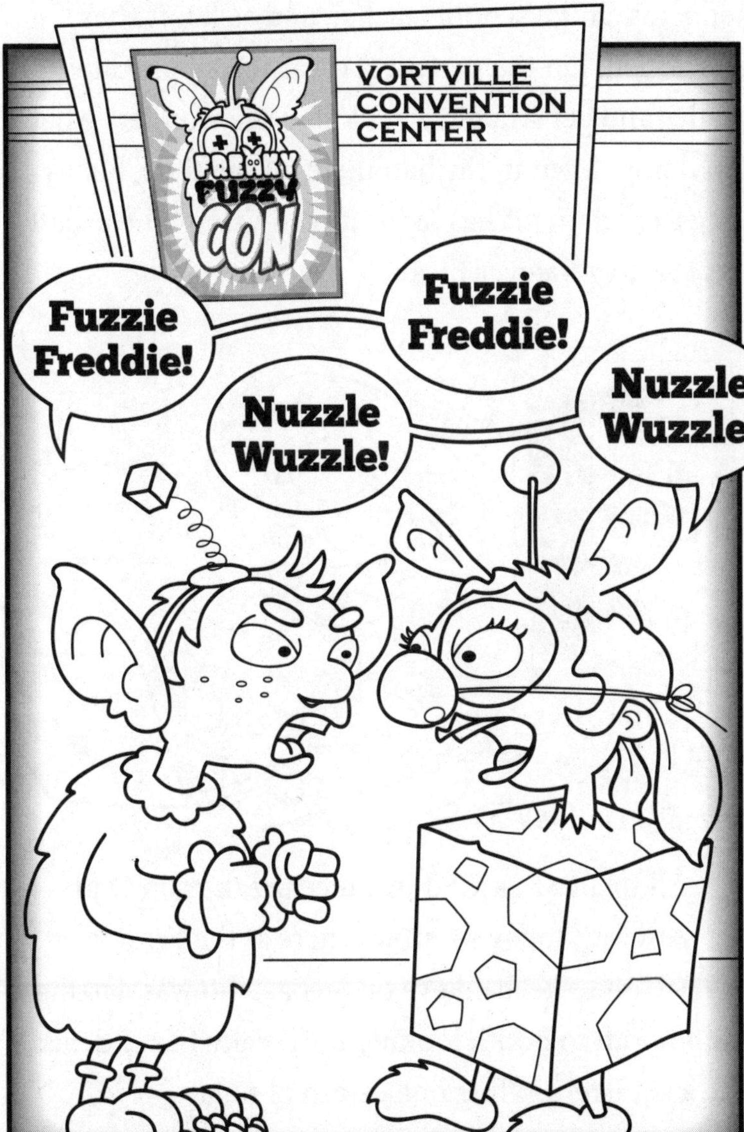
FREAKY FUZZY CON
VORTVILLE CONVENTION CENTER
Fuzzie Freddie!
Fuzzie Freddie!
Nuzzle Wuzzle!
Nuzzle Wuzzle!

I haven't told you anything about my mom yet. She's a high school teacher, and as far as she's concerned, I'm the perfect son 'cause I skipped two grades and get straight As. I know she wonders what I'm doing down in the basement all the time, but as long as I tell her it has "educational value," she usually lets me do whatever I want.

All in all, she's kind of a nice break from Dad.

Anyway, today Mom was here at the Freaky Fuzzy Con to keep an eye on Stella, who was darting from booth to booth looking for Freaky Fuzzy deals like a squirrel sniffing out a stash of nuts.

That left me and Chip mostly by ourselves to check the place out, eyes peeled for any upside-down weirdness.

But the place was packed not only with kids in costume but lots of grown-up fans in costume too. And Max Schleimer could have been any of these goofy guys dressed as their favorite Freaky Fuzzy. So Chip and I scanned the crowd, really giving everybody a close look. Was that guy's hat on upside down? Was that other guy's costume too well designed—maybe made by an architect?

Suddenly—WHAM!—I ran into what seemed like a big wall of fur. I looked up. This guy was a lot bigger and stronger looking than the others. He didn't belong here. Maybe it was Max Schleimer!

Nope. It was my dad.

"Dad!" I said, trying to keep from cracking up. He told me to keep quiet—he didn't want me to blow his Freaky Fuzzy cover. (I think he was Hairy Gary.) But his costume wasn't very good, so all these other guys kept coming over and telling him everything that was wrong with it, which was driving him crazy.

Suddenly, Dad spotted something and went into "operational mode." He whispered into a microphone in his hairy sleeve: "Subject at three o'clock! Subject at three o'clock!" Then he took off for this crowd that was forming across the convention hall. I ran after him, dragging Chip with me. Pulling my phone out, I got ready to get the C.H.I.P. on Chip's tooth up and running.

But then I saw what Dad had gotten all excited about. Some guy in a Nuzzle Wuzzle costume was break dancing and spinning on his head—*upside down*.

I grabbed Dad to stop him but he just pushed me away. So I yelled out, "It's not Schleimer!"

Everybody stopped and looked at me. Even the break dancing guy stopped dancing and fell down.

Dad looked closer at the break dancing guy then pulled me aside. He wasn't happy. "Okay, it wasn't Schleimer this time. But next time we might not be so lucky. Go back to your mother, Nort. Leave the security business to us professionals."

Dad walked off, and I felt lousy. I'd made him look kind of stupid.

Okay, he already looked stupid in his dumb costume, but I guess I'd made him *feel* stupid. But *I* felt stupid too. I reminded myself to stay on the sidelines in the future. I'd leave the *real* action to C.H.I.P.

Chapter 11
ONE STEP BACKWARD

Seth Mindwarp likes to do things big, and the Freaky Fuzzy 2.0 presentation was *big*.

With a whole bunch of costumed Freaky Fuzzy kids whooping it up in the audience, this cool light show started, and then a video came on showing the history of Freaky Fuzzies.

It first showed Seth Mindwarp as a teenager in his parents' garage, making the very first Freaky Fuzzy. He made it out of parts from his model train and an old teddy bear. The toy shorted out and burned his house down, but the Freaky Fuzzy prototype actually survived.

Freaky Fuzzies sold like crazy when they first came out, but as Seth Mindwarp got more and more successful, he also became a freak about making them better and better. He insisted that they be so "crazy fantastic" that every kid would want one.

And now, with the Freaky Fuzzy 2.0, Seth Mindwarp felt he'd made the "perfect toy."

The video really whipped the kids into a frenzy. Then, when Seth Mindwarp actually came out, everybody went totally nuts. Freaky Fuzzy fans were dying to hear him talk. And they were especially dying to see the new Freaky Fuzzy 2.0.

Next to me, Chip was going crazy just like everybody else. I asked him since when was he a Freaky Fuzzy fan, and he said since now. "They're crazy fantastic!"

This got me a bit worried. I needed him to stay focused. I mean, what if we saw Max Schleimer? I'd have to snap Chip out of it and get him going as C.H.I.P.!

Finally, Seth Mindwarp started talking, and the whole room got superquiet. He said that the Freaky Fuzzy wasn't just a toy, it was a philosophy, a vision for the future. It was about kids and machines working perfectly together.

I didn't really know what he was talking about, but it was creeping me out a little. I mean, maybe Freaky Fuzzies *were* more than just toys. After all, their first name was *Freaky*.

But Chip and I were here for security, not to buy toys. I scanned the room for Max Schleimer, but it was too dark to find anybody. (Except for my dad, who stood a head above pretty much everybody else. So much for a low profile, Dad.)

So I told Chip to look out for any signs of upside-down weirdness. Where there was upside-down weirdness, there would be Schleimer. But Chip was too into this slide presentation that Seth Mindwarp was putting on to pay attention to me. He just kept pointing to the screen onstage. So I looked, and I realized what was going on.

All the slides were *upside down*!

It was Schleimer, I knew it! I looked to the back of the theater into this control room where the digital projector was. Schleimer must be in there! He probably tied up the techy guy there, and turning the projector upside down was just his first trick. Next it would be the whole convention center!

I pulled out my smartphone and hit the commands—and Chip became C.H.I.P. right before my eyes! I made him a stuntman at first, but I knew he could switch by himself to something else later if he needed to.

After all, now he was *thinking* like C.H.I.P. instead of my computer doing the thinking for him. I crossed my fingers that everything would work right since this was the first real test where he was in control.

I told him to go stop Schleimer . . . and C.H.I.P. was off! He ran across the whole auditorium on the backs of people's seats. People didn't know what was going on at first, but then someone said, "Hey, it's that guy who stopped The Big Cheese!" and the crowd jumped up and went crazy! But C.H.I.P. didn't pay attention; he just swung on a light cable right into the control room. CRASH! (Yeah, there was this big window there.)

Sorry to **CRASH** your party!

Once C.H.I.P. got inside, he didn't find anybody—not Schleimer or even anyone who worked there. I radioed C.H.I.P. that Schleimer had probably taken off to do his big upside-down plan. Maybe he was going to attack Seth Mindwarp!

So C.H.I.P. took off for the stage!

By this point, Seth Mindwarp was totally confused and upset. His big presentation wasn't exactly going as planned. But think how upset he'd be if the whole convention center was turned upside down! I knew C.H.I.P. and I were doing the right thing.

Then I saw someone in costume jump onstage and charge Seth Mindwarp! I radioed C.H.I.P. that it was Schleimer. So C.H.I.P. tried to cut through the crowd, but it was too hard with everybody standing. So he turned into a rock star and crowd-surfed all the way to the stage!

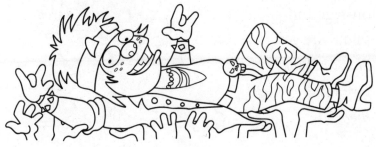

Then C.H.I.P. leapt onto the stage and ripped the costumed guy from Seth, throwing him to the floor!

Yep, it was my dad. He was trying to protect Seth. Major whoops.

Okay, I admit it—that's when I froze. C.H.I.P. was up there wondering what to do, and I didn't know what to say. I was freaking. By this point, the whole audience was cracking up—and they were laughing *at C.H.I.P.* (And I guess it didn't help that C.H.I.P. looked pretty weird dressed head to toe in red and black leather.)

And that's when this Freaky Fuzzy 2.0 rolled out onstage and said, "*Are you okay? Let me give you a hug!*"

The crowd started laughing even harder. Seth Mindwarp introduced the Freaky Fuzzy 2.0 to all the fans. And if the fans weren't excited already, now they went totally bonkers. They rushed the stage—they all wanted a new Freaky Fuzzy 2.0 of their own *now*.

In all the hubbub, C.H.I.P. slipped away, humiliated. I couldn't believe it—yesterday he was a hero, today he was a fool. Which meant I was a fool. I deactivated C.H.I.P. and got Chip out of there fast. Chip and I found Mom again and pretended we'd just gotten lost. I played it cool, trying to hide my total shame.

Then Stella ran up with her brand new Freaky Fuzzy 2.0.

I pretended to care, but I was really just thinking about C.H.I.P.—and how I almost blew it for good.

Chapter 12
AND THEN THERE WERE THREE

That night was like Christmas for almost every kid in town.

But not for me and Chip.

Kids like Stella were playing with their new Freaky Fuzzies, but Chip and I were holed up in the basement wondering what went wrong. Actually, Chip was playing the new Freaky Fuzzy video game while I did most of the worrying.

The good news, I guess, was that the new C.H.I.P. actually worked. C.H.I.P. did everything right—it's just that he did all the wrong things. And that was mainly my fault. I was in charge of a multiskilled secret agent, but I was giving him bad information.

Yeah, it was really depressing.

My dad and his team were still out looking for Max Schleimer. I knew Dad might end up destroying half the town again trying to save the other half, but I didn't trust C.H.I.P. enough anymore to feel we could help. Chip and I were stuck—almost back where we started.

But then . . . things started to get really freaky. And I mean *Freaky Fuzzy* freaky.

Stella barged into the basement. She had her

Freaky Fuzzy 2.0 with her, and it was even more annoying than her old one. While I was trying to keep Stella from snooping, the Freaky Fuzzy 2.0 was getting into everything! It was just a little weird.

But there was something weird about Stella too. She kept asking me why I didn't buy a Freaky Fuzzy of my own.

"Because I'm not a little kid, that's why!"

But she said Freaky Fuzzies weren't just for little kids. They were for *all* kids. What they definitely were *not* for was adults. I wondered where I fit into all this. I was ten years old, but I was smarter than most forty-year-olds.

Nort

Average 40-year-old

Anyway, Stella kept going on about how all that adults want kids to do is stop playing with their toys and do their homework and chores and stuff. This was weird coming from her because she *liked* doing her homework and chores.

Then her new Fuzzy said . . .

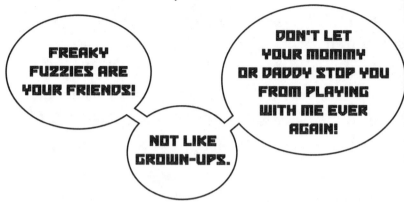

FREAKY FUZZIES ARE YOUR FRIENDS!

NOT LIKE GROWN-UPS.

DON'T LET YOUR MOMMY OR DADDY STOP YOU FROM PLAYING WITH ME EVER AGAIN!

That's when something occurred to me. I asked Stella, "Where's Mom?"

But Stella just said, "When a Freaky Fuzzy is your friend, you don't need mommies and daddies."

Then I heard this banging coming from upstairs . . . and I realized something was very wrong. Stella had locked Mom in her bedroom! And why?

Because Stella had been hypnotized by her Freaky Fuzzy!

I bolted for the stairs—but the Freaky Fuzzy tripped me! I landed flat on my face. Then I called out to Chip to help, but he didn't know what was going on or what to do. I yelled out, "The Freaky Fuzzies are taking over! Help me save Mom!"

Chip just said, "Wow!" and ran to join me.

And that's when the Freaky Fuzzy laser-blasted Chip in the butt!

There we were, Chip and I, sitting on the basement floor watching Stella and her Freaky Fuzzy move in on us like two mind-controlling robots.

"Freaky Fuzzies are your friends!" the Freaky Fuzzy said. *"Don't you want to get one of your own?"*

"Do you want me to lock you in the bedroom with Mom?" Stella asked, sounding just as freaky as the Freaky Fuzzy.

"With Freaky Fuzzies, you don't have to think anymore! Just leave the thinking to us!"

"Join us, Nort. Join us, Chip. Join us in our perfect world!"

Then the Freaky Fuzzy's eyes went all spinny, like it was trying to hypnotize us!

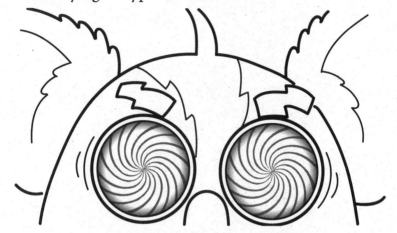

I looked over at Chip, and he was hooked. (He's kind of the suggestible type—which is why he's great at being C.H.I.P., I guess.) But then *I* started to get hooked too! I couldn't tear my eyes away from the freaky thing! So I realized what I had to do. With my last bit of free will, I pulled out my phone . . .

. . . and I activated C.H.I.P.!

Chip turned into C.H.I.P. and immediately snapped out of it. I made him a stuntman again, so he jumped up, but before he could go for the Freaky Fuzzy, it fired another laser blast at him! But he dove out of the way, doing this cool roll on the floor.

But this Fuzzy must've gone into combat mode or something 'cause it started laser-blasting him like a machine gun!

C.H.I.P. was jumping all over the room as blasts were flying everywhere, taking chunks out of the wall and ceiling. One blast even hit my computer stuff!

But C.H.I.P. finally dove down and grabbed the Fuzzy from behind. Then he *smashed* it on the hard cement floor, and its pieces went flying everywhere.

WE... LOVE... You...

Phew!

I looked over at Stella, and she was rubbing her eyes like she'd just come out of a trance. She looked around at all the holes in the walls. "What's going on?" Then she saw her smashed Freaky Fuzzy. "YOU KILLED MY FREAKY FUZZY! You couldn't stand me having one and not you, so you killed it! I'm telling Mom!"

It was all I could do to calm her down and explain that her Freaky Fuzzy had taken over her brain and made her lock Mom upstairs. Then I realized . . . all over the city, Freaky Fuzzies were probably locking parents up and taking over kids' brains!

It looked like a devious plot by Seth Mindwarp to use Freaky Fuzzies to take over the world!

But Stella still didn't believe me . . . until she saw C.H.I.P. "Oh my gosh, it's the hero guy! Right here in my house! It's really you!" I realized that I hadn't deactivated him yet. And Stella didn't realize C.H.I.P. was actually Chip. She pointed at me, saying, "My brother smashed my Freaky Fuzzy! Arrest him!"

I realized that I had to tell Stella the truth. So I pulled out my phone and deactivated C.H.I.P. And right in front of us, C.H.I.P. the stuntman turned back into Chip the school goof.

Stella froze, stunned. She didn't say anything for at least a minute. (It was a nice break, actually.)

I told her all about the microthingy on Chip's false tooth. I told her about all the things C.H.I.P. could do. And I told her that she couldn't tell anybody else, *especially* Dad.

Then Stella did something that surprised me. She didn't argue with me or say she didn't believe me.

She said she wanted to become part of our team!

She said that someone needed to stay at headquarters and man my superpowerful computer stuff while C.H.I.P. and I were out saving the city.

I was just about to totally say no . . . but then I thought about it. At the Freaky Fuzzy Con, C.H.I.P. had worked great, but we had bad information, so we blew it. What we needed was better intelligence—someone who could look up stuff while we were out chasing down the bad guys.

We needed Stella.

But first we needed to let Mom out of her bedroom. "Coming, Mom!"

Chapter 13
TEAM C.H.I.P.

We also needed to tell Dad what was going on.

Max Schleimer wasn't the crazy bad guy threatening the city (today anyway)—Seth Mindwarp was! While Freaky Fuzzies were hypnotizing kids and locking up their parents all over town, Dad was on security detail for the guy who was making all the evil Freaky Fuzzies!

And my guess was that Seth Mindwarp was *controlling* the Fuzzies, too, maybe even using them to spy on every house in Vortville!

I looked through all the broken Freaky Fuzzy parts on the basement floor and discovered at least *two* cameras, along with a ton of other crazy cyber stuff.

This guy had to be stopped!

But I realized that in this case, Dad would be better off trying to stop Seth Mindwarp first, before I brought C.H.I.P. into the action. After all, he was already at Mindwarp headquarters. All he really had to do was grab Seth Mindwarp and lock him up.

But first I had to convince Dad that Seth was the real bad guy. And we all know that I'm not very good at convincing Dad of anything.

I called Dad. He was right in Seth Mindwarp's office, and Seth was right there with him! Dad had *no idea* what was going on around town. Seth was taking over everything right under Dad's nose, and Dad didn't even know it!

Anyway, finally I just blurted out everything. He had to take Seth down fast!

Dad didn't buy it. Okay, I guess I expected that. But what I *didn't* expect was for him to tell Seth Mindwarp all about my phone call! Seth just laughed and laughed.

And then he called in his Freaky Fuzzy army.

Dad didn't have a chance. The Fuzzies zapped him and all his men, and then threw them into a super-high-tech jail cell!

When I tried to call Dad again, someone answered but just listened. I realized something was very, very wrong.

It was probably Seth Mindwarp himself!

And now he had my phone number!

This was it. Vortville was under attack *from within*. The craziest bad guy of all had infected every home in town with fuzzy toy-like viruses, pint-sized invaders that were taking over every kid's brain. And their parents were all helpless, locked up in their own homes!

Vortville needed C.H.I.P. now more than ever before!

But we needed to do more than just stop a crazy bad guy. We needed to stop an entire army of Freaky Fuzzies!

But that would be impossible! C.H.I.P. was just one secret agent! How could he stop an entire army?

Stella had the answer. "They're probably all controlled by some central computer network. Shut that down and you shut down all the Fuzzies."

I now felt confident that we could pull this off. Stella was the missing part of Team C.H.I.P.

With the three of us working together, C.H.I.P. would be the greatest secret agent ever!

Chapter 14
OPERATION: FRY THE FUZZIES

Chip and I took off for Mindwarp
Industries in the middle of the night.

It took a while because we had to stop and pump
up my front tire at a gas station. (Yeah, we were on
our bikes.) I made a mental note to build a C.H.I.P.-
mobile after this mission was over. (Check it out. It
would be totally cool!)

ONE-MILE
RANGE
NET
LAUNCHER

16-SPEAKER,
500-TERAWATT
SOUND SYSTEM

ICE-COOLED
JET
PROPULSION
ENGINE

ULTRA-
BRIGHT
MOON-BULB
SPOTLIGHT

HEAVY-DUTY
ROCK-CRUSHING
TITANIUM-BELTED TIRES

We finally made it to Seth Mindwarp's headquarters. There were no barbed-wire fences or guard dogs, but I knew the place probably had the highest-tech security around. Then I noticed something moving in some of the second-floor windows. I checked it out with my Go-through Goggles, these see-in-the-dark goggles I invented.

The things in the windows were Freaky Fuzzies! They were scanning the area like security cameras. C.H.I.P. was going to have to be extra stealthy getting inside. Seth Mindwarp probably had Freaky Fuzzies everywhere!

I asked Chip if he was ready. He said, "Ready for what?" I sighed a little and activated him with my phone.

Chip became C.H.I.P. in an instant. Wow. I felt pretty cool.

C.H.I.P. started as a supercool ninja, and he took off for the building. I could see the Freaky Fuzzies turning to watch him, but he flattened himself against the building so fast that I don't think they picked up anything. Then C.H.I.P. pulled out some Gummy Grippers, these cool suction-cup things I invented, and climbed right up the face of the building!

C.H.I.P. had a camera on the front of his suit so I could see everything he saw on the screen of my phone. It was weird with him climbing the building because it looked really scary—I'm afraid of heights. Good thing it was him up there and not me!

When C.H.I.P. got to the top of the building, he found this big vent, and he slid right down into it.

Using my earpiece, I was able to talk to C.H.I.P., but I was also connected to Stella back at headquarters. And *she* could see C.H.I.P.'s video feed too. On the computer, she pulled up a floor plan of the Mindwarp building so she could follow C.H.I.P. as he crawled through the air ducts.

I tracked C.H.I.P. on my phone as well. We both watched him sneak his way closer and closer to Seth Mindwarp's office, the nerve center of the whole Freaky Fuzzy world takeover!

Just then, Stella and I noticed something on the floor plan—another blinking light was following C.H.I.P.'s! It was a Freaky Fuzzy in the air ducts!

I radioed C.H.I.P.: "Freaky Fuzzy moving in from behind! Fifty-five yards and closing!" C.H.I.P. crawled faster, but the Fuzzy was really moving. Suddenly, the Fuzzy got in sight of C.H.I.P. and fired a laser blast! It missed, giving C.H.I.P. just enough time to tape my Ricochet Reflector to his butt. The next blast ricocheted off the Reflector's mirrored surface and shot right back at the Freaky Fuzzy!

ZZZZAP! The Fuzzy blew itself up!

As quietly as he could, C.H.I.P. kept moving, slithering farther through the air ducts.

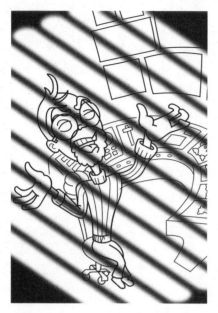

Finally, he made it to Seth Mindwarp's office. He looked right down on Seth from above, through a vent. Seth was at his massive computer console, monitoring the activity of all the Freaky Fuzzies around the city. He laughed as he snooped into nearly every house in Vortville, where the parents were all locked up, the kids were zoned out and the Freaky Fuzzies were in charge!

This was our big moment, the real test for C.H.I.P. If he blew this, it would be *serious* trouble.

I actually hesitated. I couldn't order my best friend to put his life in danger and attack the craziest of crazy bad guys!

Luckily, C.H.I.P. didn't know the meaning of self-doubt. When the time was right, he used my Zippy Zip Wire to drop down right next to Seth Mindwarp!

Seth was taken totally by surprise, and before he could do anything, C.H.I.P. spun Seth's swivel chair around, tying him up with a rope! I couldn't believe it was so easy!

That's because it wasn't.

C.H.I.P. looked around and realized the room was filled with Freaky Fuzzies! And they were moving in on him fast!

The Freaky Fuzzies started laser-blasting C.H.I.P. from all sides! C.H.I.P. whipped out the Ricochet Reflector, but it could only block some of the incoming blasts. A few of the blasts hit Seth's big computer console, and he screamed, "Watch the equipment, fuzzballs!"

C.H.I.P. pulled himself up on the zip wire again, and he spun around in midair, still deflecting the Freaky Fuzzies' laser blasts. He fried a lot of them using the Ricochet Reflector, but then one blast hit the wire itself, and C.H.I.P. fell straight down and landed hard. WHAM!

Good thing his Nifty Ninja Suit had air bags!

But now C.H.I.P. was flat on the floor and face-to-face with a mass of Freaky Fuzzies! They grabbed his arms and legs and held him down. And while C.H.I.P. tried in vain to fight them off, some other Fuzzies untied Seth Mindwarp.

The last thing I saw on my phone was Seth Mindwarp leaning in, laughing all crazy and grabbing the camera.

Chapter 15
TRAPPED

Okay, this was not good. C.H.I.P. was trapped!

I asked Stella to track him, and she told me he was being taken to another part of the building. I wondered if he had gotten free and was trying to escape. But his blinking light on my phone stopped moving. The Freaky Fuzzies had probably stuck him in the same type of super-high-tech jail cell that my dad was in, and he couldn't get out!

I panicked. What could I do now?! I couldn't go in there and save him! If they trapped Dad *and* C.H.I.P., they would definitely trap me! But I had to try, right? I mean, what other choice did I have?

It was then that I discovered I really didn't have any choice at all . . . because I was suddenly surrounded by a hundred Freaky Fuzzies! Before I could do anything, they knocked me down and started dragging me into the building!

And then I dropped my phone!

Now I was Seth Mindwarp's prisoner, and I had no way of finding C.H.I.P.!

Chapter 16
A DISSATISFIED CUSTOMER

It turned out that finding C.H.I.P. wasn't that hard 'cause we both got locked up in the same high-tech jail cell surrounded by lasers. One false move and FZZZT!

C.H.I.P. became the cat burglar who earlier broke into the Cheesemobile, and he tried to find a way out, but we were stuck for good. This was hard for him to accept since he was programmed to be  able to have *any* skill, but there was no skill that was going to get us out of this cell!

But then we heard a noise down the hall. It was the sound of someone walking, but the first thing we saw was a bunch of Freaky Fuzzies crawling along. Then, like a king surrounded by his soldiers, Seth Mindwarp appeared, and he stared right at us with his intense, beady eyes.

I could tell he was really pleased with himself. His Freaky Fuzzies were taking over the city. Soon they'd take over the world. My dad couldn't stop him. C.H.I.P. couldn't stop him. I guess he figured *nobody* could stop him now.

"Welcome to the new world order, gentlemen." Wow—he called us gentlemen. That felt kind of cool, especially since just a few weeks before I'd been called "nerdlinger" by Corey Smertz while he was stuffing me into my locker.

Seth Mindwarp went on to tell us about his big plans for his Freaky Fuzzies. He said that originally he had no intention of giving them mind-control abilities. All he wanted was for every kid in the world to own a Freaky Fuzzy. After all, it was the world's most crazy fantastic toy, right? "But parents didn't cooperate," he said. "They insisted on buying their children video games and blocks and train sets. But a child with a Freaky Fuzzy doesn't need any other toy! A Freaky Fuzzy brings hours and hours of joy! So why didn't *all* the parents *just buy it*?!"

C.H.I.P. and I looked at each other. Yep, this guy was loopy.

So this was Seth Mindwarp's plan. People don't buy your toy so you brainwash their children and take over the world. And *we're* the ones with the problem.

"But I now see that this was my destiny all along," he said. "Freaky Fuzzies aren't just toys, they are a way to save the world! In a Freaky Fuzzy world, there will be no fighting or pain or disorder. In a Freaky Fuzzy world, the whole world will be of one mind! *MINE!*"

I could see it now. A future with nothing but Freaky Fuzzies and their kid owners following them blindly. Somewhere, all the parents would be locked up, guarded by a horde of Freaky Fuzzies.

C.H.I.P. and I had to stop this. We had to stop Seth Mindwarp for good.

But how??

Suddenly, a bell went off. It sounded like a doorbell. Weird. Who would be ringing the bell of Mindwarp Industries at this time of night? Seth got all annoyed and left the hallway, followed by most of his Freaky Fuzzies while some stayed behind to guard us. C.H.I.P. and I wondered what was going on.

We couldn't see this, but it was Gert von Brugen at the door! She had a Freaky Fuzzy of her own, and it had broken down. Now she wanted a refund from Seth Mindwarp himself! Seth told her to call Mindwarp Industries in the morning and slammed the door on her.

Gert was shocked and offended. "The customer service at this company is atrocious!" But as she stormed off, she tripped over something and almost fell flat on her face.

It was my phone!

Gert picked it up, annoyed. Then she turned it on . . . and realized it was mine. "Nort McKrakken?! What's he doing here? Wait a minute . . . is he working with Seth Mindwarp?" She sat down and started to think . . .

Meanwhile, C.H.I.P. and I were trying everything to get out of our jail cell. But we were still getting nowhere. There was no way out of this place! And to make things worse, the Freaky Fuzzies were talking to us.

"Why do you want to leave?"

"Freaky Fuzzies are your friends."

"We love you! Don't you love us too?"

Then they all started looking at us with those weird eyes. They were trying to hypnotize us!

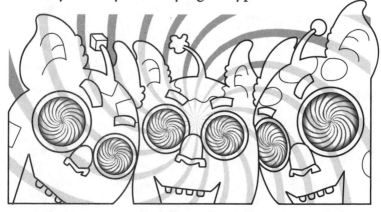

I closed my eyes and turned away. But then I noticed C.H.I.P. getting hypnotized! I couldn't believe that the Freaky Fuzzies could even hijack C.H.I.P.'s brain! I grabbed him and shouted, "Close your eyes!" So he did . . . but the Fuzzies kept on talking.

"Don't you like us? We're your friends. If you love us, you'll be happy . . . forever!"

"AAAAHHH!!!" I screamed! I couldn't take it anymore. I yelled, "I don't love Freaky Fuzzies! I hate them! Go away!" Suddenly, the Freaky Fuzzies got all confused. They started wandering around like they didn't know what to do. It's like their programming was freaking out or something.

I realized I was onto something. So I started yelling at them some more, and I got C.H.I.P. to yell at them too. We just went on and on about how much we *didn't* want them to be our friends.

And they just couldn't take it. Then they started to stray into the laser bars of our jail cell! ZAP! ZAP! ZAP! They were frying themselves, one after another!

And this was causing the lasers to fritz out too!

I couldn't believe it—the Freaky Fuzzies were breaking us out of jail!

Chapter 17
AN UNEXPECTED OFFER

Thanks to the fritzing Freaky Fuzzies, C.H.I.P. and I were out!

But we knew Seth Mindwarp would be back soon, so we had to act fast. First, we had to get back to his office to shut down the Freaky Fuzzy network. Then we had to save my dad!

C.H.I.P. and I started running, but we had no idea where we were in the building. I still didn't have my phone, so I couldn't see the floor plan to know which way to go. But we found an elevator and decided that maybe Seth's office was on the top floor.

But when the elevator door closed, we realized two Freaky Fuzzies had followed us in! And they were staring at us and trying to hypnotize us again—we couldn't look away!

Finally, C.H.I.P. did what secret agents do—he took action. Still a cat burglar, he opened the ceiling hatch of the elevator and climbed out into the elevator shaft! I thought that was so cool! . . . until I realized he wanted me to follow him. But I couldn't follow him! The elevator was still moving! *He* was the secret agent, not me! I was never supposed to be inside the building in the first place!

Suddenly—WHOOP!—C.H.I.P. yanked me up into the elevator shaft.

I looked up—we were almost at the top . . . and almost about to be crushed! But then C.H.I.P. jumped up and forced the elevator doors to the top floor open and pulled me in after him.

We made it just in time! *Phew!* Then C.H.I.P. jammed the elevator door so the Fuzzies couldn't get out of the elevator and follow us.

We'd guessed right—we had found Seth's office. And luckily there were no Freaky Fuzzies there since they were all still with Seth.

C.H.I.P. and I immediately got to work at Seth's huge computer console. Realizing cat burglars knew nothing about computers, C.H.I.P. quickly changed himself into the electronics guy who'd defused The Big Cheese's bomb.

But when we looked up at all the monitors, we almost froze. The Freaky Fuzzies weren't in everybody's houses anymore, they were all on the streets . . . and they were coming for us! And right behind them were all their kid owners, still hypnotized, moving in on Mindwarp Industries to stop us fast!

C.H.I.P. and I rushed to reprogram the computer to shut everything down . . . but then C.H.I.P. started to freak out! He suddenly morphed into the skater dude who was chasing after The Big Cheese! Then he became the chemist! And then the wrestler! What was going on?!

Finally, C.H.I.P. became the electronics guy again so at least I could get him back to working on the computer. But we had to act fast in case he freaked out again!

Suddenly—WHAM!— someone kicked the door open. We spun around, ready to take on Seth and the Fuzzies . . . but it was Gert von Brugen! "A-HA!!!" she cried as she held up my phone. "I knew you were working with Seth Mindwarp!"

"Gert von Brugen??" My voice cracked from the stress. "What are you doing here?? And how did you get in here anyway?!"

It was then that she spotted C.H.I.P., and that's when her mind really got whirring. "Wait a minute . . . you're working with the hero guy? I knew it! He's really a superandroid created by Seth Mindwarp! He's like a huge Freaky Fuzzy!"

This idea really made me sick, and all I wanted to do was tell her how wrong she was—but we had the world to save.

Then I realized why C.H.I.P. was morphing all over the place—because Gert von Brugen was fooling with my phone! I told her to give it back and let me go on shutting down the Freaky Fuzzy network.

But it was too late. Seth Mindwarp and his Fuzzies finally showed up.

In no time, C.H.I.P. and I were surrounded.

But then Gert stepped right in front of Seth with a big cocky grin on her face. He couldn't believe she was here either, and he ordered her to leave. But she said, "You shouldn't work with Nort. He doesn't know anything. You should work with me!" Gert was right— Seth *should* hire her. She was just as evil as he was!

But Seth didn't think so. He ordered his Fuzzies to drag Gert off to a laser jail cell.

When Gert was finally out of the room, Seth turned back to me and C.H.I.P. I knew it was all over. We had blown it. Vortville—and soon the world— would be completely enslaved by the Freaky Fuzzies.

But then Seth said something I totally didn't expect. "Nort, I want you to come and work for me." *Huh??* "We're alike, you and I. We're both ahead of our time, and nobody understands us. *My* father didn't understand me any more than yours understands you."

Seth pushed a button and Dad came up on a monitor, stuck in his laser jail cell.

"Look at him. No imagination. For him, might is right, and that's all there is to it. But you and I . . . we can change the world for the better!"

I couldn't believe what I was hearing. For once in my life, a father-figure-type guy actually understood me. Also, I imagined what I could do with my C.H.I.P. technology with Mindwarp Industries behind me.

But there was one problem: Seth Mindwarp was evil! Why did he have to be evil?! Why couldn't he be a brilliant tech guy who was out to do good? Maybe he had been good at one time. I mean, he invented a whole bunch of furry little toys. But then he had to go and turn them into brain-eating zombies.

Think of what he'd do with C.H.I.P.!

It was then that I realized that, even though my dad totally didn't get me and did everything in a kind of stupid way, at least he believed in doing things for the right reasons.

He didn't get me, and I didn't get him, but he was a good man, and he was still my dad.

Chapter 18
C.H.I.P. GROWS UP

This was the moment of truth.

C.H.I.P. and I knew we had to do something fast, or everything was really over. But when C.H.I.P. tried to change from being the electronics guy to a karate guy, he couldn't do it! Gert von Brugen must've messed up his programming when she was fooling around with my phone!

But then I noticed something on the floor—my phone! Gert had dropped it while the Fuzzies were dragging her out. I dove for the phone and quickly changed C.H.I.P. from the electronics guy into a karate guy!

In a cool karate move, C.H.I.P. jumped up and grabbed his zip line, which was still hanging from the ceiling. He swung over and kicked Seth Mindwarp in the chest, knocking him to the floor!

I got to work again fast at the computer console. But then the Fuzzies started to move in on me and C.H.I.P.!

We were so close to winning . . . but I didn't think we were going to make it!

Stella came up on the phone. "Where've you guys been?!" I told her I didn't exactly have time to explain.

The Fuzzies started to crawl up C.H.I.P. and drag him down! On the floor, he wrestled with them, but those things are really strong when they get together.

I realized I needed to make C.H.I.P. the wrestler again, but that's when Seth got back up and came for me! I was so nervous, I could barely work my phone!

But I finally did it, and C.H.I.P. turned into the wrestler just in time. He threw off all the Freaky Fuzzies and jumped back up. Then he picked up Seth Mindwarp and spun him around on his shoulders! Seth went cross-eyed, and C.H.I.P. hurled him across the room!

"URGH!" Seth Mindwarp was out for the count!

I knew I was supposed to be concentrating on shutting down the Freaky Fuzzy network, but I couldn't help jumping up and cheering C.H.I.P. That move was so cool!

Finally, I settled in at the computer console to shut the system down for good. Seth Mindwarp had passed out, but the Freaky Fuzzies were still a true threat to mankind. And I needed C.H.I.P. to fend them off while I worked—but I didn't know what skill he should use to do it! Something told me he needed to be something more than just a wrestler, something faster. The fact was that only *he* could change himself into what would work best, as he'd done before.

So I had to stop working at the computer console and reprogram my phone first. And all this with Freaky Fuzzies moving in on me fast!

But I fixed the code just in time, and C.H.I.P. immediately turned into a tennis pro! (See? I would've never thought of that.) He started smacking the Fuzzies away with his tennis racket, one after another, like tennis balls. (He had a really great backhand!)

But even *he* had a hard time keeping up with the onslaught of crazy furry toys.

Then the door burst open, and in came the Fuzzies from all over the city! Their hypnotized kid owners were right behind them, and they soon had C.H.I.P. and me surrounded. They were closing in fast! Nothing could stop them!

A few of the Fuzzies started getting through to us. I could feel them climbing up my legs! I was *just* about to shut down the network—but the Freaky Fuzzies were now at my arms, tugging away, trying to stop me!

Finally, I typed my last line of code, and I reached for the *Enter* button—but then one Freaky Fuzzy actually bit me!

That's when I snapped. "Get off of me, you freaky furball!"

I flung the Fuzzy across the room . . .

. . . and hit *Enter!*

Suddenly, everything went silent.

The Freaky Fuzzies stopped chanting and froze in their tracks.

And all the kids in the room (and all over the city) snapped out of their trances and rubbed their eyes, wondering where they were.

C.H.I.P. and I were both out of breath. We looked around at all the deactivated Fuzzies and confused kids. Then we looked at each other.

We'd done it! We'd saved the city . . . and the world!

Stella cheered us from my phone. Then we joined in, finally able to let go.

Game! Set! MATCH!

But something was missing—Chip. After all, C.H.I.P. wasn't *really* C.H.I.P., he was Chip, my best friend. So I grabbed my phone and changed C.H.I.P. back into Chip.

Chip was once again his lazy, silly self. He smiled and said his favorite part of the whole adventure was smacking the Fuzzies away like tennis balls.

I told him he should be proud of himself for saving Vortville . . . but I reminded him that he had to keep all this a secret. He frowned a bit but finally said *okay* . . . and that he was really hungry.

I told him I'd buy him a cookie.

Chapter 19
BACK TO NORMAL...
KIND OF

So, you save the world one day . . .

. . . and the next day, you still have to go to school.

The Vortville

VOL. LXV ...No. 12,308

HERO GUY SAVES WORLD FROM FUZZY FREAK-OUT

Hooray for the Hero Guy! While the children of Vortville were being lured away by the megalomaniacal Seth Mindwarp, a 21st

But who is this mystery hero? Where does he live? What is his favorite food? And most importantly, who is he dating? Our crack team

All everybody was talking about was how
C.H.I.P. had saved the world from the Freaky Fuzzies.
The newspapers were calling Seth Mindwarp a
twenty-first century Pied Piper who tried to steal
everybody's kids. And right there next to the articles
were security camera images of C.H.I.P. fighting
off Seth and the Fuzzies in Seth's office. (For secret-
identity reasons, I had made sure earlier to delete all
the videos with me and Gert von Brugen in them.)

Herald

DAM-AGE?
Following the leads
on local leaks - PG 3

Late Edition

Once again, my dad was really angry. He felt it was his job to stop crazy bad guys, and he insisted he would've eventually gotten out of the laser jail cell by himself and stopped Seth's evil plan. But there was nothing he could do about it. It was C.H.I.P. who had saved him. And C.H.I.P. was everybody's hero now, not my dad.

And Dad wouldn't be able to find C.H.I.P. to stop him anyway! Now *that* was the big thing everybody was talking about—where was C.H.I.P. when he wasn't fighting some crazy bad guy? Everybody had their own ideas, especially the kids at school. Maybe he lived in some secluded fortress somewhere! Maybe he sailed around on his own private yacht!

Or maybe he had some kind of secret identity where he just became someone else, and nobody knew it was really C.H.I.P.

I let people wonder.

Especially Gert von Brugen.

Gert was blabbing all over school that she knew the hero guy was actually a superandroid and that she saw everything that went down at Mindwarp Industries last night. Luckily, nobody believed her. And she still didn't know that C.H.I.P. was really Chip. And she also still didn't know that I had actually created C.H.I.P.!

But she knew I knew *something* and wasn't telling. And she wasn't going to rest until I told her everything.

I braced for the endless nagging that was sure to come.

Yes, I was *dying* to tell Carla Mawhinney—again. And Chip was *dying* to tell *everybody*—again. But we thought better of it this time. We just privately enjoyed the fact that someone I created—and someone Chip *became*—had saved the world.

And we didn't even have to destroy half of it in the process.

But also, I knew that this wouldn't be the last time the world would need C.H.I.P. There would always be crazy bad guys. And where there were crazy bad guys . . .

. . . there would always be C.H.I.P.

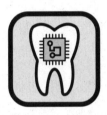

Nort and C.H.I.P. will return . . .

About the Author & the Illustrator

Richard Clark has written for many kids' TV shows on Disney, Nickelodeon, Netflix, CBC, BBC, and other foreign networks. He lives just outside of Toronto with his wife, Fiona, and their twins, Oliver and Robyn.

Rich Murray draws and animates explainer videos on topics ranging from pediatric health to cybersecurity. He lives just outside of Toronto with his wife, Mary, and their son, Nicholas.

Follow Nort and C.H.I.P., and check out more Richard Clark books at www.mybestfriendsecretagent.com, www.facebook.com/RichardClarkAuthor, and rclarkbtd@gmail.com.

Also check out Rich Murray at richtoons.com, and @richtoonstv on Twitter and Instagram, or email richtoonstv@gmail.com.

MY BEST FRIEND IS A
SECRET AGENT!

Book 2: How C.H.I.P. Took a Dive to Dash
Dr. Eelstrom's Dreams of Dunking Vortville

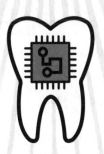

START

Secret agents **ALWAYS** have an escape route. Find your way through the maze!

Test out your **detective skills** and try to **find these words** in the scramble...

CODES   VILLAIN   SUSPECT

MOLE   SLEUTH   GADGETS

SPY   AGENT   HANDLER

CLUE   LOOKOUT   SURVEILLANCE

```
M J S S R I M Q S U Z X W I D
O Q K V Q A E C I M O H D B P
L G W I S E L T E A G E N T Y
E M B R L O O K O U T E T X N
H A N D L E R Y O L D Z C Z P
C Y M S I Y G A D G E T S H M
L W P U U Z U B I U S Q H O R
U V A R Z Y N K Y F X H C F W
E X V V X C C J D L P C I Q A
S K D E C O N R P B J K N T X
B H I I E D J T D U R P V F W
J J D L Y E J S D B H M I S F
X C S L J S J U S P Y F L V Z
Y W L A N T D S S K A F L Q W
D O E N G K B P R V P G A K V
P E U C I M N E R K K C I Z P
K Q T E N L F C O D R Q N E A
B I H W N W J T U D K K H I X
```

Secret Code Name Generator

Pick one word from **each column** to generate your secret agent code name!

TIP: Close your eyes and point to make it extra secret!

FIRST NAME	LAST NAME
Hart	Worm
Genius	Train
Bravo	Fox
Green	Bear
Purple	Flamingo
Tango	Ghost
Speedy	Cat
Silver	Thunder
Silent	Hail
Glow	Snake